WHEATON PUBLIC LIBRARY

3 5143 00524032 7

W9-ATT-595

EASY Preprimer Ballard, P

Ballard, Peg   *W*

Chad checks : the sound of
"ch"

JUL   2000

Wheaton Public Library
225 N. Cross
Wheaton, Illinois 60187
(630) 668-1374

Chad Checks

The Sound of CH

By Peg Ballard

The Child's World®, Inc.

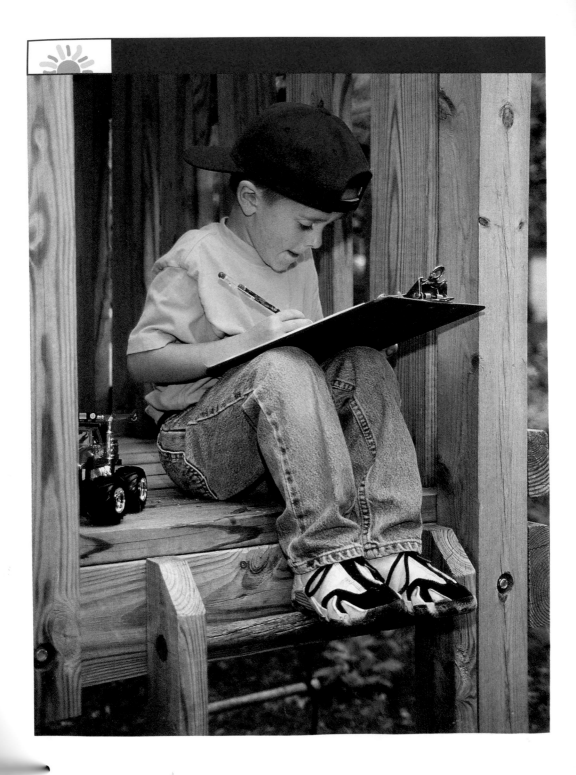

Chad checks his things.

G327

Chad checks in his
playhouse.

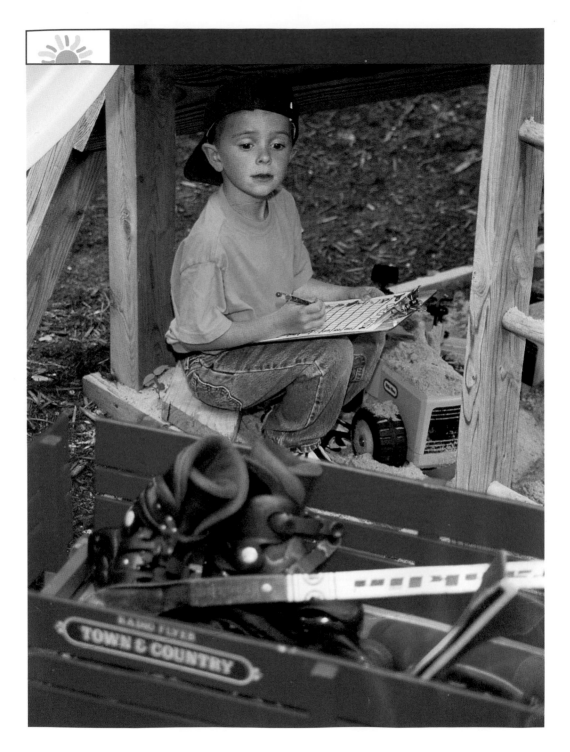

Chad checks in
his wagon.

Chad checks in
his pockets.

Chad checks in
his bedroom.

Chad checks under
his bed.

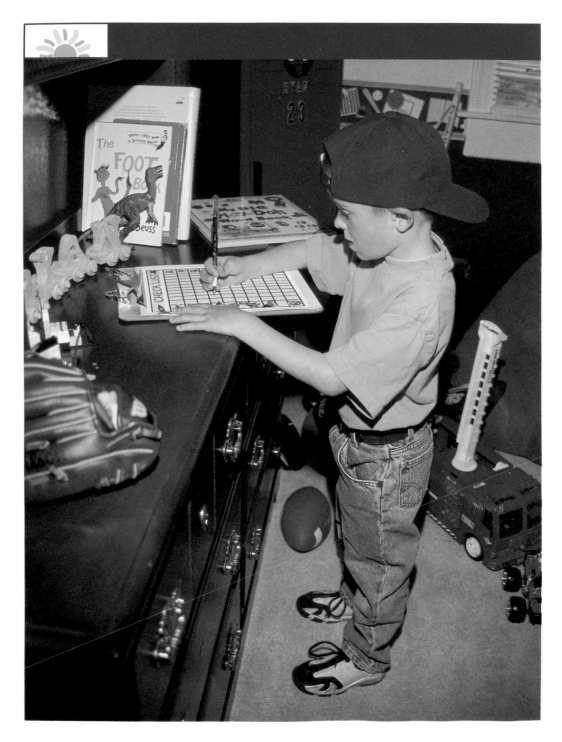

Chad checks on
the shelf.

Chad checks in
his locker.

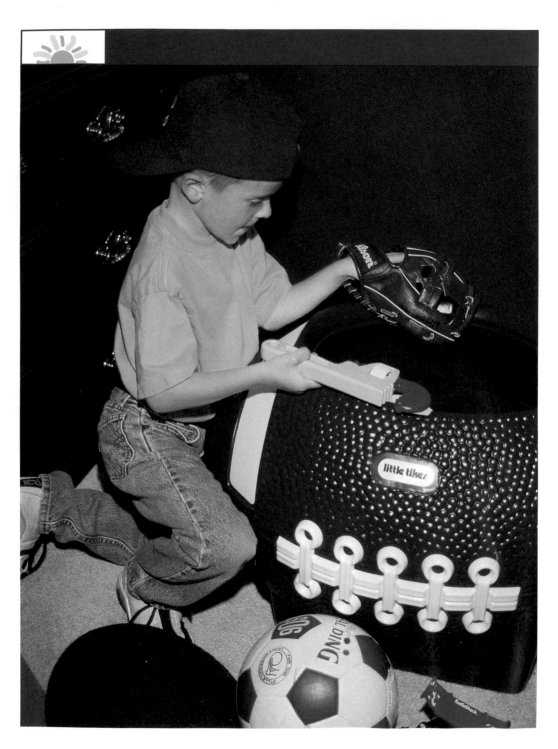

18

Chad checks in his
toy chest.

Chad will check again tomorrow.

Word List

Chad

checks

chest

Note to Parents and Educators

The books in the Phonics series of the Wonder Books are based on current research which supports the idea that our brains are pattern detectors rather than rules appliers. This means children learn to read easier when they are taught the familiar spelling patterns found in English. As children encounter more complex words, they have greater success in figuring out these words by using the spelling patterns.

Throughout the 35 books, the texts provide the reader with the opportunity to practice and apply knowledge of the sounds in natural language. The 10 books on the long and short vowels introduce the sounds using familiar onsets and rimes, or spelling patterns, for reinforcement. For example, the word "cat" might be used to present the short "a" sound, with the letter "c" being the onset and "-at" being the rime. This approach provides practice and reinforcement of the short "a" sound, as there are many familiar words made with the "-at" rime.

The 21 consonants and the 4 blends ("ch," "sh," "th," and "wh") use many of these same rimes. The letter(s) before the vowel in a word are considered the onset. Changing the onset allows the consonant books in the series to maintain the practice and reinforcement of the rimes. The repeated use of a word or phrase reinforces the target sound.

The numbers on the spine of each the book facilitate arranging the books in the order that children acquire each sound. The books can also be arranged into groups of long vowels, short vowels, consonants, and blends. All the books in each grouping have their numbers printed in the same color on the spine. The books can be grouped and regrouped easily and quickly, depending on the teacher's needs.

The stories and accompanying photographs in this series are based on time-honored concepts in children's literature: Well-written, engaging texts and colorful, high-quality photographs combine to produce books that children want to read again and again.

Dr. Peg Ballard
Mankato State University

Photo Credits

All photos © copyright: Romie Flanagan/Flanagan Publishing Services.

Special thanks to the Barth family

An Editorial Directions Book
Photo Research: Alice Flanagan
Design and production: Herman Adler Design Group

Text copyright © 2000 by The Child's World®, Inc.
All rights reserved. No part of this book may be reproduced or utilized
in any form or by any means without written permission from the publisher.
Printed in the United States of America.

Library of Congress Cataloging-in-Publication Data

Ballard, Peg.
    Chad checks : the sound of "ch" / by Peg Ballard.
    p. cm. — (Wonder books)
    Summary : Simple text and repetition of the letters "ch" help
readers learn how to use this sound.
    ISBN 1-56766-727-9 (alk. paper)
    [1. Alphabet.] I. Title. II. Series: Wonder books (Chanhassen,
Minn.)
PZ7.B21195Ch 1999
[E]—dc21   99-15890
                                                       CIP